MR DARCY

Written by Alex Field   Illustrated by Peter Carnavas

NEW FRONTIER PUBLISHING

First published in the UK in 2018
by New Frontier Publishing Europe Ltd
93 Harbord Street, London SW6 6PN
www.newfrontierpublishing.co.uk

ISBN: 978-1-912076-14-7 (PB)

A CIP catalogue record for this book is available from the British Library.

Designed by Nicholas Pike

Printed in China
10 9 8 7 6 5 4 3 2 1

For Jessica and Charlie.
AF

For Danielle.
PC

Mr Darcy lived by himself on the edge of Pemberley Park.

It was a place where the trees blossomed and the lake sparkled.

One day he received an invitation
to tea with Lizzy and her sisters.

But Lizzy lived in a small, ordinary park that
Mr Darcy never visited.

He shook his head, tossed the invitation aside
and set off for his daily walk into the village.

Everyone admired his tall hat.

As Mr Darcy turned the corner he tripped and fell
right in front of Lizzy and her sisters.

'Mr Darcy, this is a surprise,' said Lizzy.
'Are you in good health?'

Mr Darcy replied that he was in excellent health.

'Will we see you for tea on Sunday?' asked Lizzy.

Mr Darcy turned bright red. He picked himself up
and hurried away.

The next day Mr Darcy saw
Lizzy across a laneway.

Lizzy waved.

Mr Darcy quickly looked the other
way – and bumped straight into a tree.

'Are you alright?' asked Lizzy.

'Yes, just resting, thank you,' replied Mr Darcy.

'Will we see you for tea on Sunday?' asked Lizzy.

Mr Darcy turned bright red
and hurried away.

It soon began to rain and in his hurry
Mr Darcy fell in an enormous puddle.

Mr Darcy tried to move.

The more he moved the faster he sank into the thick, brown, squelchy mud.

Bingley plodded up to Mr Darcy.

'Do you need help?' he asked.

'No, thank you,' replied a polite Mr Darcy.

Lizzy and her sisters waddled by.
The sisters giggled when they saw Mr Darcy.
Lizzy asked if he was well.

'Very well, thank you,' he replied.

This time Lizzy didn't ask Mr Darcy if he was
coming to tea.

So there Mr Darcy stayed.
The air got colder and Mr Darcy
began to shiver.

Lizzy whispered a plan to Bingley.

Bingley went in search of his friends,
Caroline and Maria.

While Maria distracted Mr Darcy...

Bingley and Caroline gave
Mr Darcy one giant shove.

His hat went flying and so did he.

Mr Darcy wasn't looking quite so splendid.

He picked up his hat and mumbled
a quiet 'thank you'.

'It was Lizzy's idea,' said Maria.

Mr Darcy smiled politely and went on his way.

On Sunday Mr Darcy glanced
at the invitation to tea.

He set off across Pemberley Park,
carefully avoiding the large mud puddle.

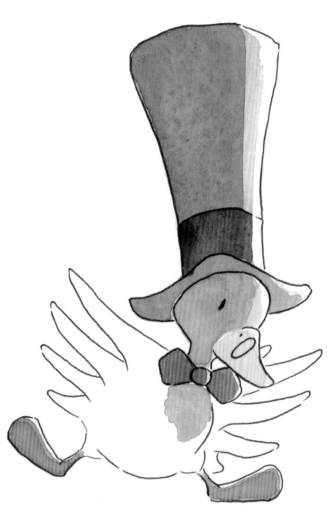

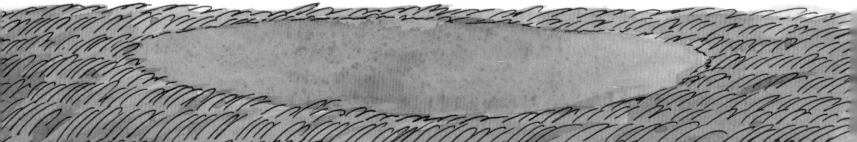

Lizzy was delighted that Mr Darcy
had finally accepted her invitation to tea.

Mr Darcy felt quite loved and not alone at all.